Let Your Heart Be Light

A Kelly Brothers Novella

(Kelly Brothers, Book 8)

by

Crista McHugh

Books by Crista McHugh

CHAPTER 1

Rupert Bates adjusted his tie and took a deep breath.

Remain focused, calm, and collected.

Unfortunately, his sweaty palms betrayed him and revealed that he was anything but calm and collected. At least he still had his focus, even though he questioned his conviction.

He curled his fingers into a fist and gave the door in front of him three efficient knocks.

Steady.

Then a dazzling smile shattered his resolve.

Maureen Kelly had to be the perfection of womanhood personified. Intelligent. Confident. Kind. Gorgeous enough to steal his breath away every time he saw her.

And today was no exception.

"Rupert," she said, the slight rise in her voice demonstrating her genuine pleasure at finding him at her door, "what a surprise."

His tie seemed to draw up around his throat like a hangman's noose, choking all the things he wanted to say to her.

She opened the door all the way. "Come inside before the wind blows you away."

Somehow, over the course of a few steps, he managed to regain his voice. Talking about the weather always served as a good icebreaker. "This is hardly a gale."

"No, but it has a definite nip to it." She peered up at the cloudy sky. "I suspect we'll get a few inches of snow overnight."

"Typical for this time of year." He came inside the warm, cheery home in Highland Park he'd visited hundreds of times over the twenty years he'd worked for the Kelly family. And just like every recent visit, a hundred pounds of white fur pounced on him.

"Jasper!" Maureen scolded, pulling her Great Pyrenees away by the collar. "Bad dog! How many times do I have to tell you not to jump on people?"

The dog simply wagged his tail and looked up at her with what appeared to be complete adoration, his tongue flopping out the side of his open mouth.

Rupert felt a twinge of envy toward Jasper. He'd probably wear a matching expression of adoration if he hadn't had years of maintaining the proper British stiff upper lip of emotional repression that had been drilled into him since he was a boy at Exeter. Instead, he shed his thick woolen coat and draped it over his arm.

"Can you stay long enough for a cup of tea?" Before he could answer, Maureen had taken his coat and was hanging it in the coat closet by the door. "I just bought a fresh tin of Assam."

His favorite tea. Of course, she knew that, just as she knew the way he liked it prepared—with a simple splash of milk. "I really don't want to be a bother—"

"Nonsense." She was already on her way to the kitchen.

"I enjoy a bit of good company."

He followed her to the massive chef's kitchen. A decade ago, it had been the hub of a large family with seven active boys. Now, it seemed cavernous and empty, belonging only to the woman who lived here alone. No wonder she welcomed company.

Maureen poured hot water into a teapot from the special spigot by the sink and measured out the loose tea leaves before adding them to the pot. "While that's brewing, what brings you all the way out here?"

If he had the courage, he would've happily replied that it was a purely social visit, but thankfully, he had the guise of work to shield him. He grabbed the file from his briefcase and placed it on the granite-topped island. "I wanted to discuss the greystone in Humboldt Park."

"We still have that property?" Maureen fetched a pair of reading glasses from the next room and perused the documents he'd laid out for her.

"Yes, and that was why I wanted to speak to you about it. Adam has plans for it."

"What are they?" She paused from reading long enough to pour two cups of tea, adding a splash of milk to his before the tea.

"He wants to tear it down and build condominiums."

Maureen choked on her tea. "He what?"

He pretended not to notice the slip in her usual poise and showed her the architect's drawing of an ultramodern structure that would house six upscale units. "The area has shown remarkable gentrification over the last few years, and he thinks we should capitalize on it."

"A condo would make sense in the city, but not there." She shuffled through the papers until she found the one she was looking for. "This home was built in 1893. It should be on the historic homes register."

"Agreed." He took a sip of the tea, savoring how she'd managed to create the level of perfection in the cup. "But the last tenants left the property in need of serious repair, and Adam thinks it would be easier to level the home and start over from scratch."

"But I love this home. It has so much character." She pulled out a photo of the exterior and pointed to the details. "Look at the masonry on the portico."

"Yes, but look at the interior." He pulled out the photos of the disaster left by the tenants. Gouged floors. Rat droppings. Grime-covered surfaces in the kitchen and bathrooms. Broken moldings and shattered windows. Water stains on the ceiling. "We'd have to gut the entire building to make it habitable."

"Then that's what we should do," she replied in a tone that offered no argument.

"But," he countered, pulling out a map of the community, "we've seen a growth in commercial properties on that street, and with the corner lot location—"

"I said no. I refuse to allow Adam to destroy a historic home."

He suspected as much, which was why he'd chosen today to go over Adam's head and approach the true owner of the property. When Michael Kelly had died five years ago, he'd left everything to his wife, Maureen. Adam may have been the face of Kelly Properties, but his mother still had the final say in any decision involving the real estate holdings.

She drummed her fingers on the counter. "Is the

building still structurally sound?"

"Yes. We replaced the roof with fifty-year architectural shingles less than eight years ago. The plumbing and wiring are still operational and up to code. No evidence of any termite damage, although, as you can see from the pictures, there is a rodent presence."

"Then it's in no danger of being condemned."

"Correct, but Adam fears the next tenants could be just as destructive." Jasper wedged in between them, prompting Rupert to rub the dog's head in acknowledgment. "A new condominium complex would command higher prices and attract those with a higher income."

"Why doesn't he just sell the place to someone who wants to restore it?"

"There's minimal profit in that."

She sipped her tea and studied the map. "The area is still considered at risk?"

"Yes, and no. West Town has shown significant growth in the housing and restaurant scenes over the last decade, and it's pushing into Humboldt Park."

"Displacing the lower-income residents in the process." She set her cup aside and rested her chin on her fist, the way she always did when lost in thought. "If a home is on the historic register's list and in sound condition, it would be very difficult to tear down, wouldn't it?"

"There would be considerable red tape to go through to obtain the necessary permits."

"Thus slowing down Adam's modern condos." She tapped one elegantly manicured finger on her cheek. "Perhaps it's time I add a few speed bumps to his plans."

Rupert grinned behind his teacup. Just as he'd suspected she would, which was why he'd chosen to pay her a visit.

They both shared the same love for historic homes. "Shall I inform him of your decision?"

"Not yet," she said with a conspiratorial grin that matched his. "Let's act before he has a chance to protest."

"Very good." He gathered up the documents and placed them back in the file folder. Now that he'd gotten the necessary business behind him, his heart pounded even harder. Decorum would suggest he should return to the office and attend to the never-ending list of tasks he needed to complete. His heart, however, wished he could linger in the kitchen with her.

"Rupert?"

Her question caught him off guard, and he stammered out, "Yes?"

"I sincerely appreciate you going out of your way to bring this to my attention."

"It wasn't out of my way at all."

"Liar. Highland Park is a considerable drive from downtown."

"It's a reverse commute at this hour," he argued before reaching into the pocket of his Savile Row suit jacket. "Besides, I stumbled across this bridge strategy and thought you might appreciate it."

She took the slip of paper with the same eagerness of a small child receiving a gift from Father Christmas. "This is wonderful! Thank you so much, Rupert."

The peck on his cheek caught him by surprise. His heart pitter-pattered with renewed intensity, and his mouth went dry. "It was nothing, I assure you."

"But you're always doing little thoughtful things like this for me."

He wanted to say it was because he secretly loved her, but once again, fear got the better of him. She was his employer, after all. "I know how much you love the game."

"This couldn't come at a better time. Emilia and I have a holiday tournament coming up this weekend and—" She stopped and stared at him, her expression drifting from puzzlement to curiosity to something he couldn't entirely read. Whatever she was feeling, it was enough to make him hope she was seeing him as something more than a friend. "Thank you again," she said softly.

"Of course," he replied, his voice still strained by fear.

He jumped back to his realm of comfort. "Shall I make an appointment for you to view the property for yourself?"

"That would lovely."

"When are you available?"

"Anytime this week." She looked around her empty kitchen. "It's not like I have to drive anyone to football practice anymore."

He pulled out his phone in an attempt to keep from pulling her into his arms and comforting her. "I have an opening in my calendar on Thursday morning at ten."

"That should work for me. This storm should blow over by then."

"But they're predicting an even stronger one this weekend." The comfortable weather talk once again washed away his insecurities. "You might want to reconsider your tournament if the roads are bad."

She responded with a disdainful snort. "A blizzard wouldn't keep me from it."

He chuckled as he added the appointment to the calendar. Maureen's love for bridge was practically legend. "Then I hope that little tidbit will be useful."

"I'm sure it will be." She pointed to the teapot. "Care for a refill for the road?"

"Yes, please."

Maureen poured the rest of the tea into a stainless-steel travel tumbler and added the milk. "Here you go."

He didn't take it right away. "I always find it fascinating that you can remember the precise way I like my tea."

"I know how you stuffy Brits feel about it, so I treat the matter with the utmost respect," she teased. "Besides, after twenty years, it's easy enough to remember a friend's preferences."

Friend. The word twisted in his chest with the brutality of being drawn and quartered.

He took the tumbler and thanked her again before turning toward the front door, Jasper following close behind. "I should get back to the office before Adam returns from his appointment. I'd hate for him to think I was doing something underhanded."

That conspiratorial grin returned as she fetched his coat. "Naturally. In the meantime, I'll call the local alderman and see if we can speed up the process on having the greystone declared a historic site."

"Very good." He donned his coat and braced himself for the icy winds that had become stronger during his short visit. " 'Til Thursday, then."

"Agreed, and drive safely." She grabbed Jasper by the collar to keep him from giving Rupert his own farewell that usually consisted of wet tongue and light covering of white fur, the modern-day equivalent to being tarred and feathered, but with affection.

Thankfully, he always carried a lint roller in his car for

his visits to Maureen. She loved that dog too much for him to mind the occasional shedding. He gave Jasper a scratch behind the ears before looking up and catching himself once again.

One day, I'll tell her how I feel.

Just not today.

He spent the entire drive back into the city berating himself for his cowardice.

CHAPTER 2

"Excuse me?" Adam Kelly asked in disbelief.

Lia, his wife of more than two years, laced her fingers through his and gave him a comforting squeeze. The relief flooding her features was the exact opposite of the shock that had tightened every muscle in his body.

The doctor sitting across from them appeared as equally relaxed. "I said your semen analysis revealed the cause of your difficulty conceiving. You have a low sperm count, Mr. Kelly."

"But-but-but…" He stammered the word over and over again as he came to terms with the news. After two years of trying to start a family, Lia had sought the advice of a fertility expert to find out why she hadn't gotten pregnant. He'd always assumed it was due to her demanding work schedule or some other reason. He'd never suspected he was the cause. "But my father had seven sons."

"Yes, but you are not your father." Dr. Upshaw, a middle-aged black woman who spoke with a mixture of intelligent confidence and no-nonsense bluntness, handed over a stack of papers with various lab results. "Mrs. Kelly is perfectly healthy. Her cycles are regular. Her hormone levels are as they should be for a woman her age. Her uterus and ovaries are normal by ultrasound. The only abnormality we found was with you."

He inwardly cringed at being referred to as an "abnormality." His whole life, he'd wanted to have a large family like the one he'd grown up in. It had taken him a while, but he'd finally married the woman of his dreams, only to face that small twinge of disappointment each month when he learned his hopes had been postponed yet again.

"As you can see, Mr. Kelly, a normal sperm count for a man your age is at least fifteen million per milliliter. Yours was nine million."

"So I'm just a little low, right?" Sweat prickled along the base of his skull. This whole time, he'd thought something was wrong with Lia. But he was the one at fault.

"Low enough to cause a problem with conception." She produced a stack of pamphlets. "The good news is that it's still possible for you to have children. I've provided some information on the causes and treatment of low sperm count—"

He winced every time she mentioned that diagnosis.

"—along with some information on in-vitro fertilization, which is a very viable option for you two."

Now it was Lia's turn to cringe. When they'd decided to seek the help of a fertility expert, she'd mentioned that she hoped they wouldn't have to resort to that.

"Is this temporary? Reversible?" he asked in desperation.

"Yes, and yes."

"Then what do I have to do?"

"We can start by doing a survey of your anatomy to make sure there isn't a physical blockage that's driving your numbers down."

Adam resisted the urge to cover his zipper. He had no

idea what that survey entailed, but he knew the anatomy that would be poked and prodded in the process.

"After that, here are a few more things to consider." Dr. Upshaw listed each suggestion by counting on her fingers. "Stress less. Sit less. Stay out of saunas and hot tubs. Keep the laptop off of your lap. Cut back on alcohol. And finally, try wearing boxers."

He was still hung up on the idea of them doing more studies on him.

Lia appeared to sense his anxiety and took the pamphlets. "Thank you very much, Dr. Upshaw. It looks like we have a lot of reading to do and a few things to discuss."

"Of course. Just let me know what you'd like to do next." The doctor shook their hands and ushered them to the door.

Adam didn't speak until they were inside the car. "I can't believe it."

"It's fine, Adam."

"No, it's not." Deep inside, he knew it was pure machismo taking control of him, but he somehow felt like he'd been emasculated in that office. Low sperm count. What was next? Low testosterone?

"So what if you're short a few swimmers?" Lisa said in a nonchalant manner.

Easy for her to say. She wasn't the defective one.

"Like she said, it can be reversed, and you *have* been hanging out in the sauna at the gym recently. Just avoid hot places and switch to boxers for a few weeks. After that, I'm sure your numbers will be higher."

She made it sound so simple, so easy. But it did little to

ease the root of his anxiety. "What if it doesn't?"

Lia sighed and looked out the window. "Then I guess we'll just have to try IVF."

Her tone told him that was the last thing she wanted. "If it's too much of a bother—"

"It's not. It's finding time to do it. I mean, you have the easy part. All you have to do is jack off into a cup. I'm the one whose body will be invaded multiple times, who'll have to take hormones that will make me moody, who'll have to carry a child while trying to run La Arietta and open the new restaurant in Lincoln Park."

He let her words sink in and realized he was asking a lot of her. If she was willing to go through all that for him, then he could go through with the anatomy survey Dr. Upshaw had recommended and settle for boxers and no saunas for a few months. "Let me do my part first before we jump to all that."

Her smile revealed her gratitude. "Thank you, Adam. If we can just wait until the new place has opened…"

"We've waited this long to start a family. A few more months shouldn't matter." But even as he said the words, a sinking feeling filled the hollows of his chest. His brothers were having children, and out of all of them, he'd been the one who wanted children the most.

And as Murphy's Law would have it, he was the one who was having the hardest time starting a family.

He pulled into the parking garage of his building on Michigan Avenue. La Arietta, Lia's award-winning restaurant, was on the top floor. Three and a half years ago, he'd walked into it determined to kick her out and make way for a celebrity chef, never knowing he'd fall head over heels for the owner. Now, he couldn't imagine a day without her.

"What's the special today?" he asked in an attempt to change the subject. He always enjoyed getting a taste of her cooking before anyone else.

She flashed him a wicked grin and replied in flawless Italian, "*Linguine ai frutti di mare.*"

"It has shrimp, doesn't it?"

She laughed and nodded. "No leftovers for you, I'm afraid," she teased, referring his allergy to shellfish, "but I think I have a nice rib eye with your name on it aging in the fridge."

"Sounds delicious." He leaned over to kiss her. "What time should I pick you up?"

"A little after ten." She leaned a little closer and whispered, "I might just have something special for dessert."

Her seductive hint shook away the last of his moping. She still desired him, even though he was "short a few swimmers."

"See you in a few hours." Lia got out of the car and blew him a kiss before ringing for the elevator that would take her to the back entrance of La Arietta.

Adam drove the few blocks that separated the Michigan Avenue building from their condo overlooking the lake. Part of him wanted to bury himself in work to forget about the news he'd received, but in the end, he decided to try to follow the doctor's advice and stress less. Maybe all this trying to have a baby contributed to his low count. He eyed the pamphlets in the empty seat next to him and wondered how many answers they might hold.

An hour later, he'd read through everything and done as

much of a Google search as he could before finally breaking down and pouring a glass of the Montepulciano that Lia had opened the night before. But when he found himself nursing a second glass, he broke down and called the one person he could turn to for advice.

His mom.

She answered on the second ring. "Hello, Adam. Did you hear the news? Sarah's expecting."

Instead of being happy for his youngest brother and his wife, the news hit him like a punch in the gut. "That's great," he struggled to say after a few heartbeats.

His mom immediately picked up on his reaction. "What's wrong, dear?"

"I—" His voice broke on him, and he took a long drink of wine before trying to speak again. "Lia and I met with a fertility specialist today to find out why we haven't been able to conceive."

His mom remained silent for a few seconds. "And?"

"Lia's perfectly fine. Healthy and fertile. The problem is me."

"Nonsense, Adam."

"No, Mom, it's true." He sank onto the sofa and confessed the embarrassing truth. "She said I had a low sperm count."

"So?" she replied. "You remember middle school biology. All it takes is one."

"Maybe so, but that doesn't explain the two years of trying." He leaned back and considered pouring a third glass of wine. If he didn't have to pick Lia up from work in a few hours, he would've been tempted to finish the whole bottle.

"Both of you are so stressed out. No wonder you're having a hard time conceiving. What you two need is a little getaway."

"The timing is bad. Lia's restaurant is so busy during the holidays, and she's working on getting the new one ready to open next month, and then I have to get things rolling on a few sites…"

"You can always make time for your wife. And if I remember correctly, Lia's birthday is coming up."

He bolted up from the sofa. *Shit!* He'd been so busy with work, he'd completely forgotten about Lia's birthday. He flipped to the calendar on his phone. Monday. He still had time.

"Maybe you should kidnap her for a little romantic getaway this weekend," his mom continued. "I hear the waters in Maui are magical, and Tom Murphy has a place in Kapalua I'm sure you could stay at if I asked him."

It sounded so simple, but the more he thought about it, the more perfect it seemed. "But what about a suitcase?"

"You can buy everything you need there. Just enjoy your time together before you start having children."

He drew in a deep breath and finally found some semblance of peace as he released it. Yes, he and Lia should enjoy their time alone together. Children would come soon enough, and once they did, it would be at least eighteen years before he had a chance to have his lovely wife all to himself again. "You think Tom will let us stay there?"

"Of course he will. He and Susan are such dear friends, and I know they aren't planning on going over there until after the holidays. I think you'll like it, too. Susan has such elegant taste."

He couldn't care less about the décor. All he wanted was a few days alone with Lia. He opened a search page on his laptop and started looking at airline tickets. "If not, I suppose we can always find a place—"

"You handle the tickets and leave the accommodations to me."

He was already one step ahead of her. "There's a flight Thursday morning that would have us there by four in the afternoon, and we can come back on Tuesday."

"Perfect! Book it, and have a great time. I'll email you directions to Tom's house after I talk to him."

She hung up, and he bought the tickets in a matter of minutes. Afterward, he texted Lia's sous chef, Julie, and asked if she'd be willing to manage the kitchen duties at La Arietta for the weekend so he could take Lia on a surprise getaway. There was no one Lia trusted more with her restaurant.

Once Julie texted back that she was in, Adam grinned.

Everything would work out in the end.

Chapter 3

Maureen pulled into the driveway of the historic three-story neoclassical greystone in Humboldt Park and parked behind Rupert's shiny black Mercedes. From the outside, it looked well kept. The bare bushes looked a little overgrown, but the snow had been recently shoveled from the sidewalks and driveway. Part of her hoped the inside wasn't as bad as the pictures suggested.

Rupert got out of the car in time to open the door for her. "Good morning."

"Good morning to you, too." She gave him a warm smile. Rupert always had impeccable manners. "It doesn't look as bad as I was expecting."

"Snow covers up a multitude of sins." He pulled a key ring out of his pocket and made his way to the front door.

She followed him, taking in the exquisite details in architecture. The stone arches. The three stories of bow windows. The massive front porch. "This looks like it was built by a Freemason," she said, pointing to the two globes on the front porch.

"One more thing to add to your arsenal, I suppose?" he replied in a dry tone while he unlocked the door. "And I suppose it was more than coincidence that Adam decided to take his wife on a surprise vacation this morning?"

"Are you suggesting I'd talk my son into leaving town so I can go behind his back and have this property declared a historic site so he can't tear it down?" She did her best impression of innocence.

Rupert, however, wasn't falling for it. "I always knew you were a clever woman."

"I have to be, after raising seven boys. Now, let's take a look inside."

The stench nearly knocked her out when he opened the door. Her stomach threatened to return the small breakfast she'd eaten that morning. "What kind of people lived here?"

"Ones who apparently lacked basic cleaning skills." Worry creased his face. "If you wish to leave, Maureen, I would understand."

She shook her head. "I need to see how bad it truly is."

Thankfully, the smell eased once they opened the front windows and aired the place out. Now she could focus on the rest of the mess. Trash left behind by the former tenants lay piled up in the corners, the likely source of the stench. Easy enough to clear out. A thick coating of dust and dirt lay over the scratches and scrapes that marred the original hardwood floors. She peered closer at them. "Is this bird's-eye maple?"

Rupert nodded without looking. "Yes, along with the trims and the upstairs mantels. All original to the home and in desperate need of refinishing."

"This inset appears original, too." She wiped the dust away to reveal the leafy, fern-like branches adorned with fuzzy flowers. "This looks like acacia."

"Another Masonic symbol, I presume?"

"I believe so, along with the fact the house faces east. But Mike was the Freemason, not me." She stood up and

19

moved toward the back of the house, forming a mental to-do list.

The chimneys needed to be inspected and cleaned.

The downstairs bathroom was hopelessly dated by the dusky pink tile.

The kitchen was cramped and equally as dated, not to mention as filthy as the rest of the house.

But it all had potential.

She knocked on a wall. "What's on the other side of this?"

"A small room that was probably intended as a bedroom."

"Can we tear it down to expand the kitchen?"

Rupert pulled out a small tablet and typed in a note. "I can speak with a structural engineer about it."

"Thank you. Open-room concepts sell homes, and I think if we open up the kitchen and have it flow into the dining room and front parlor, we could attract more buyers. We can update the bathroom and leave the extra room as a possible office." She glanced around the room one more time, envisioning her changes. "Yes, that might just work. Now, on to the next two levels."

The upstairs revealed much of the same—dirt and grime and rooms in need of modernization. Rupert said nothing as they assessed the rooms, preferring instead to deal with something on his tablet.

"Here is one proposal I've quickly drawn up," Rupert said, handing her his tablet. "This property has always been a single-family home, but many of the people moving to this neighborhood are young professionals who don't need such a massive house. It's one of the reasons Adam wanted to build condominiums here."

The drawings on the computer showed a set of three single-level flats and a basement that had been divided into storage units. Each unit had the open kitchen-dining-family room concept, along with two bedrooms that shared a full bath.

Maureen studied it. "Are you suggesting a compromise?"

Rupert nodded. "This way, we can cater to the needs of the community, increasing our potential profits by splitting it into three properties instead of one, while still protecting a historic building."

He swiped to another screen. "Here is a list of all the permits we'd require, though. They would be similar to the ones we'd have to obtain to build new structures here, but since this is already standing, they might be issued more swiftly."

She reviewed the long list, then swiped back to the drawings. "There's no chance we can keep this a single-family dwelling?"

"We could, but we'd have a more difficult time finding a buyer who'd want a four- to six-bedroom home in this neighborhood."

She studied the proposed flats a moment longer before glancing around the room. They could still maintain the historical character of the home and house more people if she went along with his suggestion. Plus, she'd be less likely to upset Adam's dream of turning this space into condos. "Let's move forward with this idea. I'll speak to the alderman about preserving this home and see if we can fast-forward the permits."

"And I'll run the plans by our engineers to make sure

they're viable." He tucked the tablet away and signaled for her to descend the stairs first.

She'd just gotten to the first floor when her phone rang. She checked the number before answering. "Hello, Emilia. Did you find a new bridge strategy for this weekend's tournament?"

"No," the hoarse voice on the other end replied. "I woke up this morning with a fever of a hundred and two. The doctor says it's the flu, and he doubts I'll be better by Saturday." A coughing fit prevented her from saying anything more.

Maureen's heart sank. Not only did she feel miserable for her dear friend, but now she would have to withdraw from the tournament she'd been looking forward to for weeks. She fought to keep the disappointment from bleeding into her voice. "You just rest and feel better. Can I bring you anything?"

"No, I don't want you to get this. Lia's stocked my freezer with her cooking, and I can always call out for pizza."

"Are you sure?"

"Yes. I just feel horrible for letting you down."

"Nonsense. It's not like you planned on getting the flu. Besides, there will be other tournaments. Call me if you need anything in the meantime."

"Thank you." Emilia hung up, leaving Maureen to finally absorb the self-pity she'd been holding back.

Rupert cleared his throat. "I couldn't help but overhear, but it sounded like you might have to withdraw from your bridge tournament this weekend."

"Emilia has the flu, poor thing." She indulged in a few

more seconds of disappointment before trying to focus on something positive. "I should send her some flowers, especially since I'm the one who suggested Adam steal her only child away for the weekend."

"A good idea." He shifted his weight from side to side and fiddled with his tie. "As for the tournament, I could step in for Emilia, if you'd like."

She paused from searching for the number of her florist and shifted her attention to him. "You play bridge?"

"I'm probably not as keen on it as you and Emilia are, but I've been known to play a hand or two in my day, as well as studying the strategy of the game."

Just like the other day when he'd brought her that tip. "Are you sure that's how you want to spend your Saturday?"

"I couldn't imagine anything more exciting."

She laughed. "You must be pretty bored to consider a bridge tournament exciting."

"You make it exciting, especially by outwitting your opponents. Besides, I get to spend the day with a lovely, intelligent woman."

His smile lit up his warm brown eyes, and her heart did a strange flip-flop. "You're making me blush."

"I only speak the truth." He opened the front door for her. "What time should I pick you up?"

"There's no need for you to bother—"

"It's no bother at all. The drive will give us a chance to solidify our strategy."

"How does eight sound? I'll have a quick breakfast whipped up for us, and we'll be able to get there in plenty of time before the tournament starts at nine."

"Sounds like a plan." He turned and locked the front

door. "It seems we both have full agendas until then."

Indeed, and part of it included sorting out the fluttering in her chest that started when Rupert offered to step in as her partner for the tournament.

Chapter 4

Maureen hugged the oversize, gaudy trophy and grinned. "Thank you so much, Rupert. You have no idea how much today meant to me."

A smile played on his lips as he recounted the day. He couldn't have cared less about winning. He'd just enjoyed the company. Winning was a bonus that made her happy, which in turn made him happy. "You came prepared to win."

"And we did." She held the trophy out in front of her and lovingly stroked the shiny surface of the cup. "Champions."

Her joy warmed him from the inside out, despite the snowy night. Traffic moved at slower pace, which gave him more time to work up the nerve to suggest dinner. But with each mile that crept by, his courage faltered. She was technically his boss. And she'd shown no sign she thought of him as anything more than a good friend. By the time he pulled into her driveway, he'd concluded once again that now was not the time to tell her how he felt.

Coward.

"Do you want to come inside?" she asked.

Her question caught him by surprise, and before he could carefully craft an excuse why he shouldn't, he found himself nodding. A few seconds later, he was scrambling out of the car to open the door for her.

"Thank you," she said as she got out, the perfect specimen of grace.

At least, until her shoe slipped on the ice.

Rupert lunged to catch her, wrapping his arms around her waist and pulling her close to him.

His breath caught when he realized how wonderful she felt in his arms.

She doth teach the torches to burn bright, he thought as he gazed down at her face.

If Shakespeare had been alive today, he might have attributed that line to Maureen, for he couldn't imagine anyone more suited for that description.

The surprise faded from her expression, melting into something he couldn't read. For the first time ever, she appeared to see him as something more than her company's right-hand man. She seemed to see him as just a man and pressed her hand over the spot where his heart frantically beat.

His blood rushed to places that threatened to compromise his secret admiration of her, so he reluctantly let her go before she could see what kind of effect she had on him. "Careful," he mumbled as he looked away.

"I guess we have a few icy patches under the snow," she said, her voice unusually high and breathy.

He looked up. In the twenty-plus years he'd known her, he'd never seen Maureen Kelly flustered. And perhaps she wasn't. Perhaps the rosy glow in her cheeks was due to nothing more than the cold. Perhaps the way she kept sweeping her hair behind her ear was nothing more than an attempt to make sure it stayed in place. Perhaps the twitchy way she pressed her lips together was her way of making her lipstick wasn't smearing. He could make excuses all night. It was far better than getting his hopes up only to have them shot down.

She sidestepped around him, her movements cautious. "Would you like a cup of tea?"

How about a shot of whiskey?

But he nodded and walked alongside her, ready to catch her if she slipped again. "Tea would be lovely."

He rested her hand on his lower arm while they navigated the fresh snow that had fallen while they were away. It covered the circular drive and the brick stairs that led to the front door, painting the world in white. Christmas was a mere three weeks away, but Mother Nature had already created the ideal holiday card image. All it lacked were the twinkling lights on the Christmas tree peeking through the window and the welcome wreath on the front door.

"I'm surprised you haven't started decorating for the holidays," he said as they entered.

"I'm still trying to force myself to do it." She scratched a sleepy Jasper behind the ears.

The giant white dog moved to him and placed several licks on his hand. He forced himself not to wipe with his handkerchief right away. "But you love the holidays."

"I do, but when none of my children can come home for Christmas, I find myself asking what's the use."

The sadness in her voice pleaded to his knight in shining armor complex, and he swooped in to rescue her spirits. "That's not entirely true. Adam will be here."

"Yes, but Frank has a game on Christmas Eve, and Ben

27

is in the middle of his season, too. Gideon is shooting a new movie, and poor Caleb might be deploying in the next few weeks, and Ethan's on tour, and…" She threw her hands up in the air. "My boys are all grown up and don't have time to come home for Christmas anymore."

A frown tugged at Rupert's mouth. If her boys could see how much their mother missed them, they would probably find some way to come home for a day or two.

"I'll probably just join Emilia at Adam and Lia's place for Christmas. It'll save me the time and expense of decorating." She pulled off her high-heeled shoes and dropped them at the foot of the staircase. "Assam or Darjeeling?"

He discreetly cleaned Jasper's dog drool off of his hand. "You wouldn't happen to have an oolong?"

"You're in luck." She pulled out the familiar teapot and filled it with hot water before retrieving a canister from one of the cabinets. "I have a fresh supply of Tung Ting."

He noted that she only added enough leaves for one cup. "Aren't you going to have any?"

"No, I'm going to have this instead." She exchanged the tea canister for a brandy snifter and a bottle of Hennessy X.O. "I'd offer you some, but I know you have to drive home."

"Are you suggesting an Englishman can't hold his liquor?" he teased.

"Certainly not." She flashed him one of her brilliant smiles and fetched another glass. "Care for some?"

"Just a smidge. As you said, I do have to drive home." Although part of him wished he could stay.

Of course, the longer he remained in her company, the

greater the risk of him exposing his feelings. And that was teetering into dangerous territory.

Once she poured him a glass, he held it in his hand and swirled the cognac around to warm it. "I wish there was a way to give you the Christmas you want."

"So do I." She stared into her glass. "But it's part of life. For almost thirty years, those boys were my world. And now…" She gulped her cognac in one gulp.

Worry revived his inner knight. "You visit them regularly. After all, weren't you just in Seattle for Jenny's baby shower?"

She nodded. "I know it's selfish of me to think I could keep them all here, but the travel is good for me. It keeps me from wallowing this big, old house alone." She rubbed Jasper's thick white fur to console him. "No, I didn't forget you," she said to the dog, adding, "Besides, it leaves me more time to devote to causes that are important to me."

"Such as bridge tournaments?" He blew on the surface of the trophy and buffed it with his sleeve.

She slid it across the counter, out of his reach, and sank onto one of the barstools at the island. Jasper huddled beside her on the floor. "And historic preservation."

"Yes, I received the notice from the city yesterday that the Humboldt Park property was now a protected historic site. You work quickly."

"It helps to know the right people." She pointed at the teapot. "Do you mind if I—?"

"Help yourself. I'm still waiting for the Hennessy to reach to the proper temperature so I can fully enjoy it."

She rolled her eyes and poured the tea. "You Brits and your propriety."

"I think of it as making sure I enjoy everything as it was

meant to be enjoyed." He stopped swirling the brandy long enough to inhale the butterscotch aromas filled with hints of citrus and dried currants. "Almost ready to drink."

"You're a very patient man."

"Yes, I suppose I am." He regarded her as she spoke. He had been patient. And he could continue to be so if it meant he could enjoy her company at the proper time. "The structural engineer reviewed the plans and emailed me a few hours ago that everything looked appropriate. Of course, we'll need to get the city to sign off on them."

Maureen grinned over the rim of her teacup. "Leave that to me. I want to have this all greenlighted before Adam returns."

"I get the sneaking suspicion you enjoy going behind his back on certain matters." He had never forgotten how she'd initially subleased the space for La Arietta to Lia for a fraction of the price it could've yielded, and then threatened to block Adam from giving the space to a stuck-up ponce of a celebrity chef.

"I have to keep the boy on his toes and remind him who's really in charge."

Although she said it in a teasing manner, the words bore their full impact on him. A subtle—and perhaps unintentional—reminder that she was his boss.

He took a sip of cognac and allowed it to burn all the way to his stomach. "Have you chosen a designer yet?"

"No, I haven't, but I want someone who can update the property while still maintaining the period character. I'd love to do a combination of a restoration with the renovation."

He listed several designers he'd worked with over the

years who might fit her needs. "But I think the best person would be Gretchen Sternhold. She's a lovely young lady who's making quite a name for herself working on some of the North Lawndale greystones."

"Then it seems I've found my designer. Once again, you've proven yourself to be indispensable, Rupert."

The compliment served to stroke his ego a bit, but still not enough for him to jeopardize his position.

They drank in companionable silence for a few minutes before he finished off his cognac. "If you'd like, I can reach out to Gretchen as early as tomorrow morning and see if she'd like to sign on for the project."

"That would be lovely. Thank you." She took his empty glass and placed it in the sink, Jasper on her heels. "But it can wait until Monday. I'm sure I've monopolized enough of your time this weekend."

"It's always a pleasure to spend time with you, Maureen."

She tilted her head to the side, wearing that same unreadable expression from earlier. The one that sent his blood rushing. The one that signaled that he might have overstepped his bounds.

Then a slow smile lifted the corners of her mouth. "The same."

The jump in his pulse must've sent the alcohol straight to his brain because his legs felt unsteady and his tongue refused to form a coherent sentence. He drew in a deep breath to regain his composure.

Focus on safe subjects. Work and the weather.

"I look forward to working with you on this project. But for now, I should probably return home before the storm intensifies."

She peered out the window. "I think it already has. The snow's getting heavier."

"All the more reason for me to leave."

He turned and made it halfway to the door before she called out his name.

"If you're worried about getting home safely, you can always stay here."

His trousers protested from the effect her suggestion had on him. He'd give anything to stay the night with her, but he regretfully knew what he had to do. "Thank you, but if I leave now, I should get home before the worst of it hits."

"If you insist." She walked with him to the door and stopped him from leaving by grabbing his hand. "And thank you again for filling in for Emilia. We should do this again sometime. We make a great team."

He glanced down at how well her hand fit in his, and his chest tightened. They would make a good team. She knew him better than anyone. She calmed him. She excited him. She left him feeling whole when he was with her and lost when she wasn't.

Yet he still hid his cowardice behind the mask of civility he'd worn for so long. "Call me whenever you need someone to fill in for Emilia."

Then he pried his hand from hers before he gave into his baser instincts and took her up on her offer to stay the night.

One day, I'll tell her.

The ache deep inside reminded him that each day he gave into his cowardice, he was losing a day with her. *One day soon*, he promised himself.

But for now, he could start by giving her the one thing she wanted for Christmas. He'd get all seven Kelly boys home for the holidays, and he'd use any means necessary to do it.

CHAPTER 5

Maureen opened up the interior designer's drawings on her phone while she rode the elevator to the main office of Kelly Properties.

Her breath caught.

Gretchen had captured her vision perfectly.

She released her breath with a squeal of delight. So far, everything was going to plan, but she also knew Adam would more than likely discover what she'd been up to this morning, which was why she decided to come into the city and rescue Rupert until her son's temper had cooled down.

The door opened, and she walked out, her attention still fixed on the sketches on her phone. She could walk to Adam's office in her sleep. It was the same office her late husband had used, and she'd probably walked a hundred miles from all the trips she'd made to see Mike when he was working.

This time, however, she ran right into a surprise roadblock.

A hand grabbed her by the elbow to steady her. "So sorry about that," the ever-polite British voice said.

She looked up at Rupert and smiled. "I would apologize, but I'll call it a pleasant surprise, bumping into you like this."

"I'd refrain from the pleasant part of it until after I meet with Adam. He just called me to his office." The worried expression on his face suggested it most likely involved the Humboldt Park property.

She refused to let him take the heat for her decision and looped her arm through his. "Let me handle this, Rupert."

"I'm a grown man, Maureen."

"And I'm still the owner of this company. It's time I reminded Adam of that once again."

Arm in arm, they walked into the office where a man in a tailored suit paced back and forth in front of the wall of windows like a caged tiger. His head snapped up when he heard the door open, his face twisted into a furious snarl, only to balk when he saw his mother. "Mom, what are you doing here?"

"I just wanted to fill you in on a few things I handled while you were on vacation." She gave Rupert a wink before releasing him and crossing the room to straighten her eldest son's tie. "And how was Maui?"

"It-it was nice," he stammered before turning to Rupert. "Bates, what the hell happened with the Humboldt Park residence? We were on course to demolish it and—"

"Adam, dear, don't yell at Rupert. Yell at me." She flicked a bit of fuzz off of his shoulder. "I'm the one who overrode your orders."

"I'm not going to yell at you, Mom."

"Then why are you yelling at him?" She sat down in Adam's desk chair, crossed her legs, and swiveled in a not-so-subtle hint that she was, indeed, still the one in charge.

"He knew what my plans were for this property."

"And thank goodness he alerted me to a possible neighborhood violation." She stilled and gave her son the

35

same sweet smile she'd given him when he was a child throwing a temper tantrum. "You see, this property has significant historical value, both as a greystone and as a prime example of Freemasonry from the turn of the century. Once the local alderman realized that, he declared it an historic site, which meant you couldn't demolish it."

Adam crossed his arms and glared down at her. "And I wonder who tipped him off?"

She played innocent. "Surely, you don't mean me?"

"We could've made a killing on that site. Dad bought it back in the seventies for next to nothing, and that neighborhood is up and coming. We need to strike while it's still hot and cater to the young professionals moving into it."

"And we are, while still preserving the home." She pulled up Gretchen's sketches on her phone again and handed it to Adam. "As you can see, I'm already working with a designer."

He flipped through the drawings, each swipe growing less and less resentful. "Did you know about this, Bates?"

"I just received Ms. Sternhold's drawings not ten minutes ago, but I'm familiar with her work on similar homes."

Adam returned her phone. "I see you're proposing we turn it into three flats."

"I am. That way, we both get what we want." She rose from the chair. "Now, if you'll excuse us, I made reservations for Rupert and me at Blackbird, and I'd hate to be late."

She nodded to Rupert as she made her way to the door. "Come along. We have so much to discuss over lunch."

Rupert gave her a smile that was a mixture of defiance and amusement. "I'd hate to upset Mrs. Kelly," he said before following her out the door and into the elevator.

Once they were on their way to the parking garage, he patted his chest. "Oh, bother, I forgot my coat."

She prevented him from pressing the button to go back up. "My car is still warm from the drive down. It's just a quick dash from the valet to the front door. Besides, do you really want to be cornered by Adam right now?"

"Not particularly."

"Then forget about the coat. Besides, it's not that cold outside. Just a brisk twenty-seven degrees."

"Which is still below freezing."

"We can warm you up with an aperitif when we get to the restaurant." She kept moving toward her car as soon as the elevator opened. "Or, if you want, you can settle for plain, ordinary tea."

"There is nothing plain and ordinary on the menu at Blackbird."

"Of course not. That's why I love eating there, too." She stopped in front of her Tesla Model D and waited a split second for the door handle to pop out. "Come along, Rupert. We have ten minutes to get there, and you know how traffic can be at this time of day."

"Just one moment." He stopped to do something on his phone before climbing into the passenger seat. "I forwarded Adam the email from Gretchen, along with the email from our engineer and the approved permits from the city."

"Nothing for him to worry about now other than writing the checks." A shiver of anticipation shimmied down her spine from the prospect of working on the home. "And thank you again for suggesting Gretchen. I met with her yesterday, and she was an absolute delight. Even better, she understood my vision for the home, and that has me so excited to begin."

"I'm very glad to be of service." In contrast to his relaxed manner on Saturday, he sat uneasily in the seat. Too rigid. Too stiff. Too restrained.

"Is something wrong?" she asked.

"No, nothing wrong. It's just that I worry that lunch may take too much time away from your other plans."

"Nonsense. I have no other plans today until two, when I'm meeting with Gretchen to look at paint and tile samples." Worry began to swirl in her stomach as she continued to watch him out of the corner of her eye. "Are you saying you don't want to have lunch with me?"

"Of course not. As you said, I love dining at Blackbird, and you already know how much I enjoy your company."

His posture said otherwise.

Thankfully, the drive to the restaurant was short, and by the time he got out of the car, he seemed to be more like his usual self. He opened the door for her and filed in behind her as they made their way to the maître d'. A minute later, they sat at their table, and the tension between his shoulders appeared to have loosened.

But it wasn't completely gone.

"What's wrong?" she asked.

"Nothing." He picked up his menu and hid his face behind it.

"I know you, Rupert, and I can tell when something is troubling you."

He lowered the menu enough to peer over it. "My

apologies, Maureen. I was inside my head for too long."

"And what is going on inside your head?"

"More than a penny's worth," he replied with a wan smile. "However, I'm looking forward to lunch."

"Consider it my way of thanking you for stepping in for Emilia this weekend. I had such a wonderful time." That strange and familiar flittering sensation restarted in her stomach as she said it. When she met Rupert's gaze, it intensified. Her cheeks flushed.

I haven't reacted this way to a man in years.

The realization unnerved her to the point that she sought refuge behind her own menu. The words all blurred together when she tried to read the list of entrees. She fought the urge to press her hand to her chest and slow the rapid pitter-patter of her heart. She was a woman in her sixties, not a silly teenager. She'd been married and widowed and still missed Mike every day. Yet lately, whenever she spent time with Rupert, she found herself facing these unnerving reactions to his presence.

The waiter appeared at their table and ran over the specials. Once he finished, she'd managed to gain control over herself. Rupert was a dear friend, and she was thankful to have him. She gave her order to the waiter and focused on remaining calm.

"I took the liberty of pulling some photos from the era of the greystone for you to look at," Rupert said after the waiter left. "I apologize for not having my tablet with me, but we can access the cloud on my phone."

She retrieved her reading glasses and slid her chair closer to his so they could share the screen. He started with pictures of the neighborhood in general, followed by family photos of a period greystone in pristine condition.

"As you can see in this one, wallpaper was very fashionable back then," he said, pointing to a colorized photo he'd found.

"Yes, but I doubt that would go over now."

"Agreed. But if you were aiming for an authentic restoration of the home, that would be something to consider." He flipped to the next photo, which was a scanned image from a ladies' magazine from the turn of the century. "I thought this was interesting because it described the popular colors for home décor at the time."

She leaned in to read the small font and caught a whiff of his cologne. It was a subtle mix of bay leaf, leather, and pepper—masculine without being overwhelming. It suited Rupert.

"I would defer to Gretchen on this matter, but many of the colors that were popular when the house was built in 1893 are coming back into fashion. Creams, slate grays, mossy greens." He flipped through a few color postcards from the period to demonstrate each color.

She nodded, unable to speak due to her acute awareness of him. It was the same sensation she'd gotten when he'd caught her the other night after she slipped. And it was only natural to feel such things when he had been holding her in his arms. But they weren't even touching right now. And yet, she couldn't shake the spring of giddiness welling up inside her.

She needed to get her mind off him before she said or did something that made him even more uncomfortable. She started by shifting her chair back to its original position, far enough away from the scent of his cologne or the warmth radiating from his body. "I appreciate the effort you've put into this project."

"Let's just say I share your passion for older homes."

The word *passion* spiked a resurgence of the heat in her cheeks.

The waiter saved her from embarrassment by bringing the first course to the table. She could easily blame the color in her cheeks on the steaming soup she sipped.

"I have a feeling these condos will be a hit," Rupert continued. "I've crunched some preliminary numbers on them, and I see us easily making two hundred and fifty thousand on each unit."

"Adam should be pleased with that." She mulled over the period photos Rupert had shown her, and her excitement about the project returned. "There's part of me that's almost tempted to sell my home and downsize to a condo."

Rupert nearly dropped his spoon. "You can't mean that."

"I said part of me. Let's face it—it's an awfully big home for just one person."

He nodded. "But there's still part of you that wants to stay, I assume."

"I suppose so." She dabbed the corners of her mouth with her napkin and held back the tears that still threatened to spill over when she remembered her husband. "Mike and I had many happy years there, and I dreamed of the day when my grandchildren would fill it, but I'm slowly coming to terms that won't be the case."

"Are you suggesting you'd rather have all seven of your sons living at home again?" he asked with a teasing smile.

That earned him a laugh from her. "No, I'm very proud of what my boys have achieved. I just wish they weren't scattered all over the place. Selfish of me, huh?"

"Not at all. You're a mother, and I believe most mothers feel that way. My mum was quite gutted when I moved to America. But we can't expect them to remain children forever, and now that they've become men, you are free to focus on other things."

"Like this restoration, I suppose?"

"And outwitting opponents in bridge tournaments." He smiled at her, and some of her sorrow faded.

Yes, she'd done her part as a mother. And now that she had more time on her hands, she could focus on the endeavors she'd always labeled as selfish in the past.

"Speaking of which…" Rupert retrieved his phone and pulled up a new file. "I thought you might find these interesting."

She looked over the new bridge strategy and grinned. Small things like this made her happy, and he knew better than anyone else how to make her smile.

When she met his gaze again, it wasn't the same flustered rush she'd experienced before, but a warm glow that left her calm and hopeful.

And wondering why she'd never realized what a gem of a man Rupert was before.

The rest of the meal did little to dull her feelings. They talked about everything from sports to tea until his phone rang during dessert. Rupert frowned when he saw the number and apologized before taking the call.

Frustration tugged at his features as he answered with a series of one-word responses, followed by, "I'll be right there."

After he hung up, he apologized again. "As much as I

hate to end our time together, it seems one of the properties in Wicker Park has some frozen pipes that require my attention. I need to run back to the office for my coat and keys."

"I understand, Rupert." She rose from the table with him and placed a kiss on his cheek, breathing in his warm scent again and jump-starting her pulse in the process. "Can I give you a ride back to the office?"

"It will be faster for me to take a cab. Besides, I'd hate to keep you from enjoying your dessert." His attention lingered on her even after she pulled away. A hint of smile shone through his normal all-business demeanor as he said, "Thank you again for a lovely meal with even lovelier company."

The flush returned to her cheeks with full force, and she pressed her fingers to them once he walked away.

After all these years, could I be falling for Rupert Bates?

CHAPTER 6

The first thing Rupert did when he returned to his office was fill his electric kettle and turn it on. He'd spent the last hour in the bitter cold discussing damaged pipes with a plumber. Right now, he needed a cup of tea.

The kettle reached the boiling point right as Adam knocked on his door. "You look half frozen."

"I am." He poured the hot water into his cup and tossed in a tea bag. It was nowhere on par with the exquisite tea Maureen served, but necessity called for convenience. "We're looking at four thousand dollars at least to fix that burst pipe at the Wicker Park property. I went ahead and gave the plumber the green light to proceed with the repairs and to invoice us for the costs."

"Thank you." Adam sat down in one of the leather wingback chairs that were reserved for clients. "When were you going to tell me about my mother's plans for the Humboldt Park property?"

Rupert's back stiffened, and warning bells went off in his head. "I wasn't under the impression I had to tell you anything at all. She is the owner, after all, and she came to this decision while you were away."

"How very convenient." Adam drummed on the arms of the chair. "If I didn't know better, I'd say there was something going on between you and my mother."

The tension between his shoulder blades doubled, but he focused on straining the water out of the tea bag and tossing it away. Did Adam know about his feelings for Maureen? "What do you mean?"

"I find it more than just happenstance that my mother suggests I take Lia on vacation the same day she applied for a historic landmark designation on that house. And she wouldn't have even known that the house was in danger of being torn down if someone hadn't brought it to her attention."

Rupert found himself walking a very tight line. "Mr. Kelly, I've worked for this company for over two decades, and I've known your parents for just as long. You were barely out of your nappies when your father hired me to assist him in maintaining the day-to-day operations for what was then in his property portfolio so he could focus on new projects. I'm still performing the same duties today, but I also haven't forgotten who is really in charge."

Adam arched a haughty brow as though to say it was *him*.

"If you wish to review your father's will, you'll see that he left all of his holdings to your mother, not you. It is her name on the deed, and as owner, she needs to be aware of certain proposals that may go against her wishes." Rupert took a sip of tea and watched his response sink in.

"So, you're admitting that you went behind my back to halt my idea."

"I am admitting that I thought it prudent to inform the real owner of the property of the proposed changes. She is responsible for everything that followed." He set his cup aside and crossed his arms, standing over his employer. "Never forget that your mother is an intelligent, vivacious, driven woman who will work around the clock for something she feels passionate about. She found a cause in that house, and she is beyond ecstatic to be able to restore it while at the same time turn it into the condominiums you thought would be commercially viable in the area. Just because she loves the historic charm of the home doesn't mean she wishes to ignore your proposal for meeting the community's and the company's needs."

Adam sat stock still, and for a brief second, Rupert worried he might be terminated for his speech.

Instead, Adam said, "You speak very highly of my mother."

"Because I know it to be true. She is a remarkable woman, which is why your father adored her. And if you forgive me for saying this, she deserves every ounce of respect you can give her. She put aside her career, her dreams, to raise a family, and it would be beyond disgraceful if you interfered with her plan now, especially since she is already upset that none of your brothers are coming home for Christmas."

Adam's eyes widened. "What?"

Even if he could give Maureen only three or four of her sons home for Christmas, it would fill her holidays with joy. And the perfect way to do that was to recruit the eldest to his plan. "Yes, your poor mother has been quite distraught with the prospect of no one visiting her for the holidays. She hasn't even started decorating the house."

"She hasn't?"

He nodded, noting Adam's distress over the news and wondering when the last time was that he had visited his mother. "Furthermore, she was musing today about selling her home and downsizing to a condo."

"She can't!" Adam bolted up from the chair. "We grew up there."

"Yes, but now you and your brothers are adults and have moved away, leaving her all alone in that massive house." He moved around his desk, cup in hand, and unlocked his computer screen. "Perhaps if you and your brothers gave her a reason to hold on to such a large home, say by filling it up for Christmas, she might consider holding on to it."

Adam approached the desk in a slow saunter. "What are you up to now, Bates?"

"Me, sir?" He nodded toward the screen. "I'm looking at the property values for your mother's home. She could make quite a profit on it."

"Don't you dare tell her that."

"Then I suggest you speak with your brothers and come up with a way to convince her to hold on to it."

Adam backed away, his eyes narrowed in challenge. "I will."

Rupert gave him a polite smile that toned down his inner glee at manipulating his boss into doing something that would make Maureen happy.

Together, they would give her the holiday surprise she wanted.

Chapter 7

Maureen inched along with rush-hour traffic on the Edens Expressway, humming along with the Christmas carols on the radio. Her meeting with Gretchen had been far more successful than she'd imagined. They'd unearthed a beautiful antique claw-foot tub that would be perfect for one of the units. Afterward, they found a gorgeous tile that would add a modern touch to the bathroom and add to the harmonious fusion between historical and modern that they hoped to achieve. Finally, they agreed on using exquisite Shaker-style cherry cabinets for the kitchens. And with each decision, she grew more and more excited to start the renovations.

Then "I'll Be Home For Christmas" came on the air, and without warning, she teared up. The thrill she'd known moments ago vanished, leaving an empty ache in its wake. No one would be coming home for Christmas this year.

Her loneliness continued to grow as she thought about going home to her empty house. A tear fell down her cheek.

Stop feeling sorry for yourself, her mind scolded. *You're stronger than that.*

She pulled a tissue from her purse and checked her reflection to make sure she hadn't earned a pair of raccoon eyes from her mascara. Then she instructed the Bluetooth in her car to call Emilia.

When her friend picked up, she asked, "Do you have any dinner plans tonight?"

"Nope. I just got home."

Maureen checked the GPS screen for the estimated arrival to Highland Park. "How about meeting me at Abigail's in twenty minutes?"

Emilia laughed. "Do you have a reservation for that place?"

"Not yet, but I can get one." Sometimes it was good to make friends with the hostess.

"You know everybody, don't you?"

"No, but I'm always open to meeting new people. See you in a little bit."

She hung up and dialed the café, getting their names on the list after a short, sweet conversation with Kara, the hostess and one of Gideon's former classmates.

Emilia was waiting for her when she arrived, and a few minutes later, they were sitting at a table in the packed restaurant.

"Are you feeling better?" Maureen asked after they'd given their orders.

"So much better. And I was thrilled to learn that you won the tournament this weekend. I was so worried I'd let you down."

"It wasn't as if you'd asked to get the flu. Besides, Rupert was an absolute darling for swooping in to rescue me. I admit, I was a little worried at first because I didn't know how well we'd play together, but once the game started, it was like I'd been playing with him for years."

"Rupert?" Emilia leaned closer. "Isn't he the man who works for Adam?"

"He is, and he's been such an angel lately." She started talking about the property she was restoring and all the help he'd given her. Before she knew it, they'd finished their dinners and had been handed the check.

Emilia gave her a knowing smile. "You sure think highly of Rupert."

"Of course, I do." The heat crept up her neck and jaw. She wanted to blame it on a menopausal hot flash, but after today, she wondered if it was due to something else.

Time to move to the subject she'd wanted to discuss with her friend. "Emilia, did you ever consider dating again after Paul died?"

Her friend blinked rapidly several times before shaking her head. "I was a single mom with a young child to support. There was no time for dating."

"Even after Lia grew up and moved out?"

"By then, I was too set in my ways," Emilia answered with a laugh. "But I suspect that's not the case with you."

Maureen's heart fluttered again as she thought of Rupert. "Maybe, but I can't shake the guilt of having feelings for another man. Mike was the love of my life, and we had so many happy years together."

"Do you really think he'd want you to spend the rest of your life alone?" Emilia dropped her voice into a conspiratorial whisper. "Especially when there's someone out there who obviously makes you happy?"

She twisted her wedding ring around her finger. Would Mike be upset if she dated Rupert? The longer she thought about it, the more her initial guilt slipped away. Mike had always thought highly of Rupert. Surely, he would give any relationship she had with Rupert his blessing.

But what about her boys?

The touch of a hand on hers pulled her from her thoughts. She looked up to find her friend wearing that knowing smile again.

"I understand what you may be feeling, what may be holding you back, but listen to your heart, Maureen, and pray on the matter. You'll get your answer."

She squeezed her friend's hand. "Thank you."

Maureen signed the check and rose from the table. "And while I'm praying, I suppose I can throw in a few prayers for Adam and Lia."

"Tell me about it. I've been praying for grandchildren since they got married." Emilia made a light-hearted sign of the cross. "Here's to hoping their trip to Hawaii will have been fruitful."

They laughed together and made their way to the parking lot, where Emilia gave her a farewell hug. "You're a good person, Maureen—don't ever forget that—and you deserve whatever happiness you can find."

"I just need a good friend to remind me of that." She waved good-bye to her friend and drove home.

When she walked into her house, the only greeting she received was the insistent nudging from Jasper to be let outside after being cooped up indoors all afternoon. But she ignored him and paused in front of the family portrait hanging over the fireplace. It was more than twenty-five years old. In it, Gideon, her youngest, was still in diapers. But her attention lingered on the handsome, smiling man standing behind her with his hand on her shoulder, and her eyes stung with tears.

"Please give me a sign, Mike," she whispered.

CHAPTER 8

"I know Jenny's pregnant, but she'll only be six months along," Adam argued with his brother, Dan, over the phone. "Sarah's pregnant, too, and she's coming."

"But work is crazy, and I have call that would need to be covered…"

"Did I mention Mom is talking about selling the house?"

His younger brother seemed to snap to attention. "What?"

"You heard me. She's all down because none of you were coming home for Christmas and is saying things like the house is too big for just her."

"But we came last year."

"And Jenny was just as pregnant then as she is now." Adam leaned on his desk and sighed. "Please, Dan, even if it's just for Christmas Day. I arranged for a chartered flight for Frank to bring him and his family up early Christmas morning and take them back to Atlanta later that night. I can do the same for you."

A polite knock pulled him from his conversation. Bates stood in the doorway with a file folder in hand. The second Adam nodded for him to enter, he placed the folder on his desk and departed.

"Let me talk to Jenny, then."

"Thank you." Adam hung up and put a check mark next to Dan's name. So far, he'd recruited Ben, Frank, Ethan, and Gideon into coming home. Caleb was still waiting for permission from his commanding officer for leave, but at least he'd get most of his brothers home for the holidays.

He opened the file folder to find Bates had already booked travel arrangements for each of his brothers who said they'd be there, right down to chartered flights for the ones who were still professional athletes in the middle of their respective seasons. They'd only be able to stay for the day, but his chest puffed up with pride to see they were making the effort. And just like he'd hoped, Bates had managed to schedule the arrivals while his mother would be at mass.

He carried the folder with him to Bates's office, only to catch the man as he was in the process of leaving. "Going somewhere?"

"Yes, Mr. Kelly," Bates replied while donning his coat. "I have to check on the progress at both the Lincoln Park and the Humboldt Park properties."

"Lia's been pretty nervous about her new restaurant being ready to open on time."

Bates tucked his scarf into his jacket. "Why do you think I'm making a trip there and reminding the contractors of their agreed-upon deadline?"

"I don't know what I'd do without you." Adam held up the folder with his brothers' itineraries to give as an example. "Thanks for all your work on this."

"I know how much it means to your mother." He started for the door, then paused. "Am I correct in understanding that this is meant to be a surprise for her?"

Adam nodded. "And since I have the sneaking suspicion

you'll be meeting her at the Humboldt Park house, please keep it that way."

Bates tapped the side of his nose with his finger twice and winked before leaving the office.

Adam returned his office and stared out over the city skyline. Two weeks ago, he'd been in the air to Hawaii, and even though he was glad to be back home, there was still a part of him that longed to be in that tropical paradise once again. But with Christmas only being eleven days away, he needed to pull everything together for the holidays. He'd never realized how much work it involved and wondered how his mom managed to do it year after year without pulling her hair out.

The Christmas lights twinkled along the streets below, reminding him that his mom hadn't even bothered to decorate her house this year. A frown tugged at the corners of his mouth. Mom always made a big fuss about the holidays, from the years of special ornaments she'd collected during his childhood to the fresh pine garland draped along the fireplace mantle. Home wouldn't feel like Christmas without those things.

He started to ring for Bates to have him order a tree and all the trimmings for his mom, but caught himself. Not only was Bates busy elsewhere, but if all those things showed up on his mom's doorstep, she might get suspicious. Best to probably wait and talk his mom into placing a few decorations up. Maybe this weekend...

He shifted his focus to the never-ending stack of work that needed his attention, and before long, it was time to pick up Lia from La Arietta.

She was waiting for him in the garage when he arrived.

Worry churned in his gut. Usually, she was still in the kitchen at this time, finishing up the cleaning and going over her sales for the night. "Are you sick?"

She shook her head, but when she climbed into the car, her movements appeared heavy with fatigue. "Long night. Julie offered to wrap things up for me."

He reached over and pressed his hand to her forehead. "You feel a little warm."

"I just left the kitchen." She gently pushed his hand away and fastened her seatbelt. "I wonder if I picked up something from Ma."

"Do you think she's still contagious? I mean, it's been two weeks since she was sick."

"I don't know. I just feel…off." Lia leaned her head back against the headrest and closed her eyes.

Adam considered the possible causes for Lia's malaise as he drove home. Stress. Long hours. Residual jet lag. Low B12 or thyroid. But no matter what he came up with, there was always that one hopeful explanation.

"Lia, when was your last period?"

She popped her head up, her green eyes filled with confusion. "I think four weeks ago. Let me check."

She opened an app on her phone. "Yes, four weeks ago as of yesterday."

His heart pounded as he drew the conclusion he'd been hoping for. "Which means you're one day late."

Some odd emotion flickered across her face. He couldn't tell if it was hope or fear or surprise. "I'm not pregnant, Adam."

"You could be."

"I'm not." She closed her eyes again in an attempt to end the conversation.

"Prove it," he challenged.

"Fine. I'll pee on a stick and prove you wrong when we get home," she replied with her eyes still closed.

When they arrived at their condo, she went straight to the bathroom and opened the door a couple of minutes later. "Start the timer."

They'd been through the drill so many times already, he had a timer programmed into his phone. He activated it and pulled her into his arms. "No matter what, I love you."

"I love you, too." She kissed him and added, "And who knows. Maybe you're right."

"It would be nice to not have to bother with IVF." He chuckled as he remembered what his mother had said about the waters in Maui being magical. "Maybe our little vacation was just what we needed to set everything in motion."

She chuckled, but her eyes darkened with desire. "Maybe we need to bring a little bit of Hawaii into our home."

"I'd be fine with that," he answered, fondly remembering the passionate nights they'd had there.

The timer beeped.

He met her gaze and saw the same anxious anticipation in her eyes. Hand in hand, they entered the bathroom and peered down at the small white piece of plastic.

Lia's shoulders slumped in disappointment. "Negative." She picked up the test with a wad of toilet paper and threw it away. "I told you it would be."

He kissed her forehead. "We'll keep trying."

"I know. But right now, I just want to go to sleep." She slipped past him and changed into the old T-shirt she liked to sleep in before crawling into bed.

Adam leaned on the bathroom counter and stared at his

reflection. Was it so selfish of him to want a child? Could they still be happy without kids?

Frustration leached whatever energy he had left. He stripped off his clothes and crawled into bed, cradling Lia in his arms long into the sleepless night.

CHAPTER 9

Rupert frowned as he walked up to Maureen's front door. It was a week before Christmas Eve, and she hadn't even bothered to hang a wreath. Very unlike her.

Which made his visit all the more necessary. Even though he'd agreed to keep Adam's plans a secret, he refused to let the Kelly boys come home to a house that wasn't filled with its usual holiday cheer.

He wiped his hands on the only pair of jeans he owned and rang the doorbell.

Maureen answered, wearing a soft, fuzzy jumper that matched her eyes. "Rupert, what are you doing here on a Sunday?"

"I was dropping by to help you pull out your holiday decorations." He pointed to the seven-foot fir tree on top of his Mercedes. "I even took the liberty of bringing you a tree."

"Really, that's quite unnecessary—" She was cut off by grabbing Jasper by the collar before the rambunctious dog tackled him.

"On the contrary, I think it's very necessary. You've been moping, Maureen, and I decided you needed a little holly and plum pudding in your life before you turned into Ebenezer Scrooge."

That earned one of her brilliant smiles. "I suppose you're right, Rupert. I have been moping."

"Then let's remedy it."

"Give me a moment to put my snow boots on." She invited him inside while she donned her wellies and coat. "Is that a balsam fir?"

"It is."

"My favorite." Her smile widened, and she marched out into the snow.

His chest puffed up with pride. She'd recognized his attention to detail. "I wanted to make sure I picked the perfect tree for you."

Together, they cut the ropes binding the tree to the car and dragged it to the front porch, Jasper barking excitedly between them. After a few quick shakes to remove most of the snow on the needles, they brought it inside.

He didn't need to wait for directions on where to place it. Decades of holidays with the Kelly family had shown him the treasured spot for the Christmas tree.

Maureen laughed as he leaned it against the wall in the corner of the living room, next to the fireplace. "You didn't bring a stand for it, did you?"

"No, because I knew you already had one." He swept up the fallen needles with his shoe. "And I apologize for the mess."

"It's part and parcel of the holidays." She doffed her coat and kicked off her boots. "Do you mind helping me bring down the Christmas stuff from the attic?"

"It would be a pleasure."

They spent the next half hour shuffling boxes around until they found the ones they needed. At one point when she touched his arm, he caught a glimpse of surprise. A shy smile followed, and his pulse quickened. Moments like these gave him hope that she saw him as more than just an employee.

More than just a friend.

They were pouring water into the stand's basin when the doorbell rang again. Maureen didn't have a chance to answer it before Adam's voice filled the entryway. "Mom?"

"In the living room, dear." She knelt to tighten the screws holding the tree in place and wrapped the tree skirt around the stand. "Look at the beautiful tree Rupert brought over."

He turned to find his employer standing slack-jawed in the doorway with a five-foot Scotch pine in his arms, ignoring the excited mass of white fur hopping in front of him. "Bates, you didn't tell me you were bringing a tree."

"I suppose I should've informed you that I was taking it upon myself to ensure your mother was in a proper holiday mood." *And at least I remembered how much she preferred firs over pines.*

Adam assessed the extra tree with a wry smile. "I suppose this isn't needed, then."

"Nonsense." Maureen rushed to his side and placed a kiss on his cheek. "We can make room for it in the dining room. I even think I have an extra tree stand in one of these boxes."

While she searched through her supplies, Adam sent him a puzzled glance.

Rupert did his best to ignore it. What he did in his free time was none of his employer's concern. But no matter how hard he tried, he couldn't completely squash that inner fear that Adam would find out about his feelings for

Maureen.

"Here we go." Maureen pulled an older tree stand from a box and motioned for Adam to follow her into the next room. "Let's give this tree some water."

Adam followed her, but he cast one more questioning glance as he left.

Rupert ran his finger along his collar. Now would be as good a time as any to leave, but whenever he considered the cowardly route, his blood burned. After years of playing the part of a friend, he was finally making some headway. Maureen seemed to finally see him as something more than that. And if he ran away now, he might as well kiss his progress good-bye.

So he decided to up his game.

By the time Maureen and Adam had returned, he'd turned on the sound system, piping Christmas carols throughout the lower level of the house.

Her eyes sparkled. "I'm finally starting to get into the holiday mood."

"Good," he replied, handing her a box full of ornaments, "because a light as bright as yours should never be dulled."

"Oh, Rupert," she said with a bashful giggle before taking the box and carrying it to the tree.

Adam watched the exchange between them, his expression unreadable now.

Anxiety wrapped around Rupert's gut and squeezed it.

"I know this isn't all your Christmas stuff, Mom," Adam said at last. "Bates, can you help me bring down the rest?"

"Of course." He followed his employer up the stairs, reminding himself that he had every right to be here.

Adam didn't speak until they were safely within the attic and out of earshot from Maureen. "What are you doing here?"

"I suspect the same thing as you." He made his way through the stored treasures, searching for the other boxes. "I was quite distressed to find your mother hadn't even bothered to decorate for the holidays, so I decided to nudge her in the right direction."

"I want my brothers' arrivals to be a surprise."

"They will be." He found a box and pulled it from the shelf. "And now, they will have the Christmas they've come to expect from your mother, even though she's not aware of what lies in store for her."

Adam caught him by the arm as he tried to escape the attic. "Tell me the truth, Bates. What were you doing here?"

He longed to tell Adam that his mother was a grown woman, a widow of more than five years, and could do whatever she pleased, but that reply lay lodged in his throat like a wad of poorly chewed steak. "I'm here to help an old friend whose family had become too busy with their own lives and families to check in on her."

Adam took a step back as though he'd been slapped. He released Rupert's arm, his expression a mixture of ire and guilt. "I'm here."

"Yes, and perhaps I should've mentioned to you my plans beforehand, but I know you are busy with your wife and trying to coordinate everything else for the holidays, and I wanted to help where I could." He sidestepped Adam. "Now, if you'll excuse me, I believe your mother would appreciate having her favorite Nativity scene set up on the side table to the left of the fireplace."

CHAPTER 10

Adam hung back while his mother and Bates laughed over the tangled strings of holiday lights and Jasper's attempts to add to the chaos. A strange feeling formed deep inside his chest as he watched them. He hadn't seen his mother this happy since his father was still alive.

Bates knew what kind of tree she preferred. He knew where she traditionally placed her decorations. He knew how she liked her coffee. He knew what her favorite take-out order was, as evidenced by the lunch he'd had delivered to the house. He knew how to draw a smile from her. And he knew how to revive the joy he'd been missing in her since his father had passed away.

But it was more than discovering how well Bates knew his mother. It was the secret glances he'd caught them exchanging. The shy smiles and the discreet yet innocent touches that provoked a sense of warm intimacy between them. They'd been friends for years, but lately, he was beginning to sense that they were treading into new territory.

The problem was, he wasn't quite sure how he felt about it. He wanted his mom to be happy. And Bates was a man he respected, who treated his mother with respect. But his loyalty to his father's memory prevented him from fully embracing the idea of them as a couple.

The joy in his mother's face as she teased Bates about being too OCD in the way he spaced the lights served as a swift kick to his gut. He was being selfish to think his mom would never move on and find love with another person.

But what would he tell his brothers? Would they feel the same? Adam doubted Ethan or Gideon would have any problems with Bates. Neither should Ben, Caleb, and Dan. Out of all his brothers, Frank might be the hardest to win over since he had been so close to their father and the most gutted over his death.

He waited until his mom stepped out of the room to make a pot of tea before approaching Bates. "You've done her a world of good."

Worry flickered across his face. "I have?"

Adam nodded. "Keep up the good work."

It was his way of giving them his blessing.

Then he made his way to the kitchen and rubbed Jasper's back. "It looks like Bates has everything under control," he told his mother. "I'm going to go home and whip up a dinner for Lia."

"She's not working tonight?"

"She worked the brunch shift, but decided to take a night off. The long hours and holiday rushes are zapping her energy."

A hopeful smile started to appear on his mother's face, but he cut it off before she jumped to conclusions. "And no, she's not pregnant."

The negative test the other night still mocked him. Lia was still late, but she continued to attribute it to stress.

"Then be a good boy and take care of her." She kissed

his cheek. "And don't worry so much. Amazing things happen when you least expect them to."

He wasn't sure if she was referring to his hopes of starting a family or her blossoming relationship with Bates, but he nodded just the same.

"It's Beginning to Look a Lot Like Christmas" came on over the speakers, and she bounced with glee. "Appropriate now, don't you think?"

He breathed in the scents of cinnamon candles and pine boughs, absorbed the lighthearted beat of the song, and soaked in the familiar decorations and trimmings that turned his family's home into something grand for the holidays. "Absolutely."

He waved to Bates as he left. "See you in the morning."

And as he made his way to his car, he found himself whistling along with the tune that was playing inside.

CHAPTER 11

Maureen stood behind Rupert and admired the crackling fire he was stoking. "The perfect finishing touch."

And yet, as she glanced around the living room that was draped in holiday cheer, her heart sank. It didn't chase away the loneliness. It just reminded her that her boys wouldn't be home this year.

Rupert noticed. "You're not allowed to pout at Christmas," he scolded.

"Hard not to do this year."

"Then please allow me to cheer you up." He took her in arms and swayed to the soft music playing the background.

She rested her head on his shoulder without giving it a second thought. It seemed so natural, so comforting.

So perfect.

The butterflies in her stomach started to make a return, only to be squashed when she realized what song was playing.

"I'll Be Home for Christmas."

And without explanation, she started tearing up again.

Rupert hugged her as they danced. Even without looking her face, he knew she was upset.

"This was my mum's favorite song," he murmured. "My father was in the army during the war, and she said she played the Bing Crosby recording so many times that first Christmas he was away, she ruined the record."

Maureen chuckled and lifted her head to look at him. "And let me guess—she bought a new one?"

"You forget this was during the air raids when such luxuries were hard to come by." His face split into a grin. "She bought every bloody copy she could find on the black market."

She laughed again.

"Whilst some women would do anything for a pair of silk stockings, my mum only wanted the comfort of Bing." The twinkle in his brown eyes chased away the last of her gloominess.

"Any reason why?"

"She said it was because his voice reminded her of my father's." He picked up the pace of his dance steps and started singing along with the song. "*I'll be home for Christmas, If only in my dreams.*"

He was so off key that she couldn't help but laugh again.

"Obviously, I didn't inherit my father's voice," he said with a shrug.

The song switched over to "Baby, It's Cold Outside," and he easily transitioned into a brisk foxtrot.

"You may not have a career as a singer, but you are an excellent dancer, Rupert."

"And here I thought all those dance lessons I was forced to take during my teen years were complete bollocks." He leaned forward until his nose touched hers in a playful manner, the corners of his eyes crinkled from grinning.

"Such language!" she declared as she fanned herself.

They laughed together and continued to dance around the living room.

It was the most fun she'd had since…

Since the bridge tournament two weeks ago.

And suddenly it hit her. She was falling even harder for him.

Only this time, she lacked the guilt she'd felt earlier.

"Maureen?" he asked.

That was when she realized that they'd stopped dancing. She looked up at him. "Rupert, I…"

Her courage fled. *What if I'm reading too much into this? What if he only wants to be friends?*

His hold on her loosened, and he stepped back, his gaze focused on their shoes. "I should probably go. I have work in the morning and—"

She silenced him by placing her hand over his heart. The frantic beat matched her own.

Their eyes met, and she caught a glimpse of the same uncertainty, the same longing.

He reached out, his fingertips grazing her cheek, and stared at her as though she was the most beautiful woman in the world.

It was just the confirmation she needed before rising on her tiptoes and brushing her lips against his in a hesitant kiss.

A second later, he reciprocated with a kiss at least ten times more passionate than hers. His strong arms tightened around her, pulling her close. Every touch spoke of yearning, of love, of things she'd never expected from him and yet felt as natural as breathing. Youthful giddiness pounded through her veins, awakening the desire she'd long thought dormant. She wanted him.

She might even be in love with him.

But all this left one unanswered question. How long had he been hiding his affection for her?

When their lips finally parted, they were both breathless.

Doubt clouded his expression, and he started to pull away until she stopped him again.

"Stay," she whispered before kissing him again.

Chapter 12

Rupert woke before dawn. At first, he experienced nothing but the same bliss he'd fallen asleep to, holding Maureen in his arms. She'd been every bit as passionate as he'd expected her to be, and by the end of the night, they were both left sated and exhausted.

But panic soon followed.

He'd slept with his boss.

Or to be more precise, he'd slept with his boss's mother.

Not that she needed to force him to. The moment she asked him to stay, he gladly accepted. And the adrenaline pumping through him stemmed not from her but from the fear of what Adam would say if he knew. He'd probably be sacked.

Sweat beaded along his hairline, and he rolled out of her bed, taking care not to wake her. The alarm clock read 4:13 a.m. With any luck, he could make it home, shower away her scent, and report to work extra early. Adam would never have to know.

As soon as he thought that, disappointment tempered his movements. He didn't want this to be a one-night thing. He wanted weeks, months, years of this. He wanted to marry her.

But would Adam—and his brothers—give them their

blessings?

He was in the process of pulling on his trousers when she murmured his name and sat up.

"What are you doing?"

He froze, his stomach forming one big nauseated knot. By some sliver of luck, he managed to nod to the clock. "I need to get ready for work."

"This early?"

"I have to go home and change." He rushed out of the room, frightened that if he dared to linger, he'd never want to leave.

She called after him. Jasper chased him down the stairs, but he kept running until he started his car and drove away.

Coward!

Fresh snow blanketed the barren streets. In a little while, the plows would come through and mar their beauty, but the scene comforted his frazzled nerves.

He loved Maureen.

He wanted to marry her.

But first, he needed to make peace with the men whose father he'd be replacing.

And that terrified him even more than proposing to her.

He began to solidify his plan as he drove home. Thankfully, her sons would be home for the holidays. Perhaps he could invite them out for a pint and ask their permission. At one point, he found it somewhat hilarious that he'd even bother to ask them before her. Maureen was an articulate, strong-willed woman who'd never needed a man's permission to do anything. But at the same time, it might go over better with her children if he at least made an attempt to express his love for her to them.

Shite! He couldn't even speak those words to her. Even

when he came, he couldn't utter those three words he knew in his heart to be true. *Damn English repression of emotions.*

The hot water of the shower beat down on him as he considered his options.

He needed to tell Maureen he loved her before he did anything else.

After that, he needed to decide what to do next—bring up his proposal to her first or her sons.

Of course, he'd have to find a ring.

And figure out what to say.

And pray he wasn't jumping to conclusions just because she'd asked him to stay the night.

By the time he arrived at work, he was a jumble of nerves. He couldn't focus on his to-do list. The words on his screen blurred together until he couldn't even read his email. He jumped every time his phone rang until he finally did the unthinkable and turned it off.

I can't live like this, he thought as he raked his fingers through his hair.

It was almost noon, and he'd accomplished nothing.

And then all hell broke loose.

"Rupert," Maureen said from the doorway of his office, "we need to talk."

His mouth went dry the second he saw the ire written on her face. He'd only seen her angry a handful of times—mostly when one of her sons had gotten in trouble. Usually, it was Frank who drew this intense of a reaction from her. But the idea that he'd done something to earn that unyielding glare frightened him to the core.

He rose from his chair, his knees on the verge of collapsing, only to have her wave him down.

She closed the door and stood on the other side of the room, her arms crossed. "You left in quite a hurry this morning."

He stumbled over his words as he tried to rationalize his act. "I had to work today."

"You ran away."

"No, I didn't. I—"

"Don't lie to me, Rupert." She looked away, her face twisted in disgust.

Each throb of his heart delivered a blow to his conscience. "Maureen, please…" he began, but words failed him.

"I thought you could be someone special," she said, bitterness lacing her words. "I thought you cared. And I was foolish enough to fall for it."

"I do care for you, Maureen."

"Then show me." She didn't blink as she issued her challenge.

He stood frozen, unable to find the right words when he needed them the most. He wanted to fall to his knees and beg for forgiveness, but she never gave him a chance.

"I thought as much," she said with profound disappointment and turned to leave.

"I *do* care," he repeated. He ran around his desk to demonstrate it with a passionate kiss, but she stopped him by holding her hand out in front of him.

"Are you lying now? Or do you lack the conviction to say what you truly feel?"

He tried to answer, but all that came out were a few incomprehensible stutters.

"Either way is unacceptable." She flicked her gaze from his head to his feet and back again. "I want more. I deserve more."

She left the office, slamming the door behind her.

Rupert's head swam, and he stumbled into the nearest chair before he fell from the vertigo. He'd had paradise within his grasp, and he had been too much of a coward to possess it.

And he doubted he'd have a second chance.

A knock sounded at his door.

He looked up, hopeful she'd reconsidered and returned.

Instead, Adam strolled in. He took one look at him and paled. "Are you okay, Bates? You're not having a heart attack, are you?"

He replied with a snort of laughter. Oh, the irony of that statement. His heart was breaking, but he doubted it was as fatal as what Adam feared. "No need to call the aid car."

"Are you sure?" Adam placed a hand on his shoulder and studied him with worry. "You don't look well."

He fell back on the one safety net he had at his disposal—dry humor. "I'm still recovering from your mother's visit."

"That's why I'm here. I heard she'd come into the office."

"And she left, but if you hurry, you might be able to catch her in the garage."

Adam released him and took a step back, but then reconsidered. "What happened?"

He drew in a deep breath. If he wanted to have any hope of winning her back, he needed allies, starting with the man standing before him. "We had a misunderstanding."

"About what?"

Rupert rose to his feet. It was time to be a man, not a

coward. And maybe—just maybe—if he could voice his feelings to her son, then he wouldn't fail the next time he saw her. "I'm in love with your mother."

He'd expected his declaration to be met with surprise or outrage. Adam, however, simply nodded. "How long?"

"Years."

"Why now?"

He'd once read that ninety percent of the things people feared never came to fruition. And fear had been holding him back too long. Now that he knew he wasn't in danger of being sacked—at least, not by Adam—he lifted his chin and said, "Because I've come to the realization that I'm tired of hiding my feelings."

Adam paced the room, his chin in his hand, saying nothing.

Rupert's confidence waned. Perhaps he had crossed the line. "Mr. Kelly—"

"Adam." His employer's correction was as sharp and firm as any general's order. "Call me Adam."

He hadn't addressed him as that since Adam had started working at Kelly Properties. Once he'd become Rupert's boss, he'd turned into "Mr. Kelly."

Now he had permission to address him as an equal. Rupert relaxed and allowed a smile of relief to form on his lips. "Adam, then."

The other man continued to pace. "If the slamming door I heard was her reaction to your misunderstanding, then you've pissed her off."

"Regretfully."

"But cheer up. I know a thing or two about asking forgiveness from a woman." Adam stopped and grinned. "After all, it's how I won Lia back."

"I would appreciate any assistance you can give me." He paused and voiced the one concern he had left. "You wouldn't be offended if I asked your mother to marry me?"

Adam blinked several times as though he were coming to terms with the concept before finally shaking his head. "If yesterday was any indication, you two would be very happy together."

"And would your brothers feel the same?"

He appeared to ponder the question, perhaps assessing each of his brothers' reactions. "If they can see what I've seen, then, yes. But before you start worrying about them, you have a more critical issue to tend to."

Maureen. "Any idea how I can convince her to forgive me?"

"It would help if I knew what upset her."

The awkward unease he'd dreaded entered the conversation. There had to be a way to handle it discreetly. "She, um, accused me of lacking conviction."

"Then you need to figure out a way to tell her what you've told me. But first, let me try to prime the pump for you."

Rupert arched a brow. "How so?"

Adam's grin widened. "Leave Mom to me. By the time you catch up to her, she'll be ready to hear what you have to say."

"Thank you." Rupert grabbed his coat and started planning the best way to ask for a second chance. The weight of fear had finally been lifted, and his heart felt as light as the falling snow. Now, nothing would hold him back.

CHAPTER 13

Maureen slammed the door of her house behind her and threw her gloves and purse on the sofa in disgust.

Jasper cowered in the corner, knowing better than to approach her when she was in this foul of a mood.

I can't believe I was so stupid, so gullible.

Rupert's deception tore at her heart like twisting knife. What made it all the worse was that she'd actually fallen in love with him. Somewhere along the way, he'd stolen her heart.

And now he'd trampled all over it.

She wanted to throw something else, but her hands were empty.

The Judy Garland version of "Have Yourself a Merry Little Christmas" playing in the background only added insult to injury. She wanted to be like Tootie in the film, angrily smashing a snowman because she couldn't have the Christmas she wanted.

The clock in the kitchen read a little past one in the afternoon. Not too early for a shot of something. She surveyed the liquor cabinet and settled on good old-fashioned single malt whiskey. She'd filled her glass and was raising it to her lips when her phone rang.

A curse sat poised on the tip of her tongue, but she

silenced it by downing the amber liquid. It burned all the way to her empty stomach.

Her phone kept ringing—annoyingly so. She retrieved it from her purse and checked the number.

Adam.

At least it wasn't Rupert.

"Yes, dear?" she asked when she answered.

"I heard you and Bates had a falling-out this morning."

Her cheeks burned, and she pressed her free hand to one of them to cool it. How much did Adam know about what happened last night? "I'd hardly call it that," she replied, her voice tremulous.

"It doesn't matter. I had a talk with him, and you don't have to worry about that happening again."

Her breath hitched. "What did you do, Adam?"

"I took care of things."

Fear froze away the embarrassment she'd burned with moments ago. "You didn't fire him, did you?"

"He's been going behind my back on matters for months, and now, he's upset you—"

"Adam Michael Kelly, you have no right to fire Rupert. He's been with us for years, and just because we had a personal disagreement doesn't change the fact that he is a thoughtful and considerate man whose loyalty to this family goes unquestioned."

The doorbell cut her off from the defense of the man she'd been fuming at moments before. She crossed the house to peer out the window and see who it was.

Instead of the UPS man, it was Rupert standing on her front porch.

"I'll talk to you later," she said. "Right now, I have to

clean up your mess."

She opened the door to find a penitent-looking man outside.

"I came to apologize," Rupert said.

"Come inside."

He shook his head. "Not until I unburden my heart."

She crossed her arms against the bitter cold and nodded for him to continue. She'd reinstate him, but first, she wanted to hear what he had to say.

"You had every right to say what you said earlier today, but I wish to clarify something." He shuffled his feet, his attention focused on the ground. "I was never lying, and it wasn't so much that I lacked conviction. I feared the outcome."

"Rupert, I know Adam—"

"No, please, let me finish before I go right back to where I started." He lifted his face so he was staring directly at hers. "I love you."

She tried to trap her gasp of surprise by covering her mouth, but she was too late. He loved her?

"I have for years, even before I had any right to," he continued. "And once I did, I told myself I needed to give you space, time to grieve, time to let the loss of your husband dull so you could possibly open your heart to me. I waited patiently, falling even deeper in love with you every moment I was blessed with your company."

He took a step toward her. "But as the weeks went by, I worried that you might not ever feel the same about me. I worried that you saw me as nothing more than a friend, that I would overstep my position if I dared to tell you how I felt. But today, I saw the thing I should've feared all along." He took her hand in his. "Losing you."

Tears welled up in her eyes, but unlike yesterday, they had nothing to do with missing her family.

"I know I can never be the man Michael was. I can never replace him, and in truth, I don't want to. I witnessed how much you loved him. All I'm asking is that you make a little place in your heart for me."

The tears spilled over, robbing her of speech. All she could do was nod.

"So you will give me another chance?" he asked, his face lighting up with hope.

She nodded again before kissing him.

He responded with the same passion as the night before, and her heart overfilled with joy until it spilled over from her eyes and down her cheeks.

She laughed from the absurdity of it all and ended the kiss sooner than she would've liked. But now she finally had the words she couldn't share before. She wiped her face with the back of her hand. "I love you, too, Rupert."

"Then you have made me the happiest man in the world." He pulled her into his arms and held her as though he would never let her go.

And for the first time in weeks, she forgot all about her loneliness and grief. Her heart was aglow with love and joy.

This was going to be a merry Christmas after all.

Chapter 14

Adam groaned as the incessant beep of his alarm roused him from sleep. It was Christmas morning. Thirty years ago, he would've been up at the crack of dawn, eager to see what Santa had brought him. Today, he fought the urge to crawl back under the covers.

"Wake up," Lia whispered in his ear. "*Buon Natale.*"

God, he loved when she spoke Italian to him. It aroused him as much as seeing her naked body stretched out beside him. "Merry Christmas, indeed."

He was just about to kiss her when his phone rang.

He cursed when he realized it was Caleb's ringtone.

"Highway to the Danger Zone" continued to play until Lia giggled and pushed him away. "I'll let you talk to your brother."

As she stood up, she wobbled and froze, steadying herself on the side of the bed.

"Are you okay?" he asked, worry replacing the annoyance over the snippet of the song that kept replaying from his phone.

"Just a little dizzy, that's all." Her color returned to normal, and she walked toward the bathroom without any signs of instability.

Once he knew she was fine, he answered the phone.

"What, Caleb?"

"I got leave," his brother shouted over the loud noise in the background. "Hopping a flight now. We'll be there by noon."

The rest of the conversation was lost due to the din, but he replied, "Call me when you land."

The connection ended, but at least he'd gotten the most important part. The last of his brothers were coming home, and his plan was ready to launch. Thanks to Bates's help, all of his brothers would be arriving between ten and noon while his mother was at mass. Lia's mom had even gotten in on the surprise, offering to drive her to the church and keep her away until everyone had arrived.

He bounded out of bed and dashed to the bathroom to share the good news with Lia.

She was leaning on the counter, her face pale.

"Lia?" he asked, his glee fleeing.

"I decided to check one more time. You know, since I'm still late." She held up the pregnancy test. "It's positive."

All the blood rushed from his head. Now he was the one looking for something to stabilize himself. "You're pregnant?"

She nodded and smiled. "Merry Christmas, *mi amore.*"

He wrapped his arms around her and held her close. They were going to have a baby, and he couldn't have asked for a more perfect gift. "Merry Christmas indeed."

Chapter 15

"Thank you for being so understanding," Emilia said as Maureen turned onto her street. "I'm so embarrassed that I lost my wallet. I remember it being in my purse when I left the house this morning…"

"It's fine." Maureen gazed out the window at her neighbors' homes decorated with garlands and lights. It was a scene straight from a Christmas card. The added number of cars parked along the street reminded her that this was a time for families to come together.

The disappointment that her home was empty this year didn't hit her like a punch in the gut anymore, but it still ached deep in her chest. Thankfully, they'd be on their way to Adam and Lia's after this, so she wasn't spending Christmas alone.

A smile lingered on her lips as she mentally added one more to the table. Rupert would be there, too.

Emilia thanked her again as they pulled into the garage. "Do you mind helping me look for it? I have no idea where it might've fallen out of my purse."

"Of course." She turned off the car and followed her friend inside. "I'd say we start in the living room."

"Surprise!" a chorus of voices shouted the second she walked into it. "Merry Christmas."

Her heart jumped into her throat, and she stumbled back. Then, bit by bit, she realized what she was seeing. Her entire family stood there—all seven of her boys with their spouses and children. And at the center of all was Rupert.

Jasper rushed toward her and pounced. Thankfully, the blow helped her find her voice. "What? How?" she asked in disbelief.

Rupert stepped forward. "I knew how much you missed them, so Adam talked them all into coming home, even if it was just for a few hours."

"It was Bates's idea," Adam countered. "I just used my big-brother persuasive powers, and he did the rest."

"I just can't believe…" She looked at each and every face of those she loved. "Thank you all so much!"

They all gathered around her with hugs and kisses and holiday wishes. She cherished every second of it, especially a chance to spend time with her grandchildren. And as she looked at Jenny and Sarah—both of whom were undeniably pregnant—her heart pounded with joy at the prospect of more to come. Neither Caleb and Alex nor Ethan and Becca were ready to start families like their siblings, but it was just a matter of time. And maybe Adam would get his wish soon, too.

Soon, the mouthwatering smells of Christmas dinner filled the air, mingling with the sounds of merriment. She'd been longing for a full house again, and she'd gotten her Christmas wish.

After she'd had a chance to visit with everyone, Rupert pulled her aside and asked if she'd like to join him outside. The air was crisp and cool, but the empty porch was relatively quiet. She drew in a deep breath and released it.

"This has been the best Christmas present ever, Rupert." She kissed him and cuddled in the warmth of his arms. "Thank you."

"Well, there's one more present for you." He held up a small box.

Her heart pounded as she opened it. Inside was an antique sapphire ring. "Rupert?"

He dropped to one knee. "Would you do me the honor of marrying me?"

Everything had happened so quickly, and she waited for that trigger of warning, that little voice that would tell her they were moving too fast.

But it never came.

Instead, she beheld the man before her and replied without an ounce of doubt, "I'd be happy to."

"Wonderful. Now, if only my knees felt as young as my heart." He grunted as he rose from the porch, drawing a laugh from her.

"You're not that old," she teased before kissing him.

"Mom, where are—" Gideon barged in on them, drawing to a sudden stop when he spied them together. His finger pointed to each of them in disbelief. "Wait a minute—you and Bates?"

"Is there a problem with that?" she challenged.

He shook his head and grinned. "Nope, not at all."

"Good, because I finally convinced your mother to marry me."

She playfully elbowed Rupert. "You make it sound like you asked me multiple times."

"In my head, I did." He smiled at her. "Thankfully, you said yes the first time."

"Don't keep this news to yourself." Gideon ushered

them inside. "Hey everyone, Bates and Mom are getting married."

Cheers of congratulations followed for the next ten minutes, but it never surpassed the light that filled her the moment she said yes. By the time the excitement died down, she could pick up the faint strains of "Have Yourself a Merry Little Christmas" again, only this time, she didn't want to throw a tantrum.

She was having the merriest Christmas she could imagine.

ℒETTER FROM THE ᴀUTHOR

Dear Reader,

Thank you!

Thanks for reading Let Your Heart Be Light. I hope you enjoyed it!

· Would you like to know when my next book is available? You can sign up for my new release newsletter at www.cristamchugh.com, follow me on twitter at @crista_mchugh, or like my Facebook page at http://facebook.com/cristamchugh.

· Reviews help other readers find books. I appreciate all reviews, whether positive or negative.

· You've just read the eighth book in The Kelly Brothers series. The other books in the series are *The Sweetest Seduction, Breakaway Hearts, The Heart's Game, A Seductive Melody, In the Red Zone,* and *Here All Along.* I hope you enjoy them all!

Thanks,
Crista